Rare Jewels
Publishing Company...

Black Romance
Church Drama

*M*eagan's *Fools*

Paradise - A Baptist Minister in Crisis: A

Short story

Books by Eddie Johnson:

www.EddieJohnson.net

Copyright © 2017 Eddie Johnson

ISBN: 978-0-9827188-6-5

Chapter One

Life was great for Damita Crutchfield a professor for a local upstart Ferdinand Jean University. Megan Hightower a former best friend of Damita applied to join the staff. Damita was headed from the administration building as Megan left the office.

"Hi Megan. It's been a long time since we last met."

"I know. The last time we spoke Damita was almost a decade ago, you were on your way to college in Miami."

"I teach social science here at the University. I'm headed to my first period class. Why are you here?"

"I just interviewed for a history professor position."

"Good luck. It would be nice to have you as a colleague."

"Let me get your cell number," Megan said.

"Okay. I only have a moment. Are you ready?"

Megan quickly entered Damita's number into her call phone. "I'll call you later."

Eddie Johnson

A reverse phone number look up on the internet provided Damita's address.

Megan knocked on Damita's door at first twilight. A well-built specimen of a man answered.

"What are you doing here?" Megan asked.

"I could ask you the same question," he said.

"I'm here to see Damita."

"She should be pulling into the driveway soon. Would you like to come in?"

"Okay. I guess it couldn't hurt."

"I'm finishing dinner. Would you like anything to drink? Perhaps some water or tea... I do have some chardonnay. Maybe wine is what the lady would prefer."

"No, I wouldn't care for anything right now."

"Excuse me, Megan. I'll be right back."

After a few minutes Terrell returned from the kitchen.

"Terrell Crutchfield this is a real surprise. We met the summer after we graduated high school. Our steamy eight weeks of lust and sex cannot be forgotten. I was still living at home with my parents. Your butt was bad. Your parents had thrown you out. I practically lived at your apartment when I was not home. So. Are you married to Damita?"

"Yes. We've been happily married for two years. You're probably aren't aware I'm now a minister."

"You!" Megan exclaimed. "Terrell Crutchfield a minister!"

"I'm the senior minister at Tabernacle Baptist Church."

The phone rang. "Hello. Terrell speaking."

"I am sorry baby. Do you recall the domestic violence luncheon I mentioned?"

"Yes. And..."

"Well. It's today. I won't be home for about four hours. I love you."

"I love you too. Your friend, Megan is here. I told Megan that you'd be home soon. She decided to wait on you."

"Tell Megan to call me tomorrow. I'll check my schedule. We'll set a time to meet."

"Okay Damita. I'll give Megan the message. Enjoy your luncheon," Terrell said.

"Bye baby." Damita disconnected."

Eddie Johnson

"You probably overhead me on the phone. Damita called to inform me of a luncheon that she'll be at for the next four hours."

"What type of luncheon?"

"It's a fundraiser luncheon being hosted by The Irene Haywood Foundation. Damita serves on the board of directors. Monies collected will go towards building a safe house for women caught in domestic violence relationships."

"I'll give Damita a call tomorrow."

"Good she'll be expecting your call."

"I guess, I'll see you around," Megan said.

"Would you like to join me for dinner? I hate to eat alone. I prepared for two."

"It's probably not right. But I could never say no to you."

"Give me a moment, I'll be right back."

"I would like to freshen up a little."

"The bathroom is down the hall." He pointed the way.

Terrell was now questioning his judgement. He thought to himself: *I'm wrong. I shouldn't have asked her to stay for dinner.*

Megan's Fools Paradise

Megan would sit patiently in the family room reminiscing about their past involvement once she returned.

"Dinner is served." Terrell announced.

Megan followed Terrell back to the Dining area and noticed a well-prepared dinner. He had brought out the bottle of chardonnay. "Having a little wine is not a sin.

"Oh," she snickered. "I have applied for a professor position at Ferdinand Jean University. I'm hoping to land the job, so I can be on staff with your wife, my old friend Damita. We were once the best of friends."

"Really?" Terrell scratched his head. "I never knew. I mean – Damita never mentioned you."

"And you wouldn't have known. Damita and I were never together in your presence," Megan explained. "You and I didn't really get tight with each other until after high school; and Damita at that time was busy getting ready to go off to college."

Their taboo impromptu dinner lasted approximately an hour. Megan loaded the dishwasher as a show of appreciation. Terrell retired to the family room.

When Megan rejoined Terrell romantic music was playing. She poured them each another glass of wine. Terrell and Megan slow danced. Mouths touched. Bodies shuddered. Terrell drew Megan even closer. A warm impassioned kiss followed. The music stopped.

"I really should go now," Megan said. "This isn't right. We shouldn't be getting intimate." Terrell relinquished his grip. "Thanks for the dinner."

Terrell walked Megan into the great room. He removed Megan's jacket from the coat rack by the door. He assisted Megan in slipping it on. She shivered as he opened the door. A slight chill was in the air. Terrell saw Megan out to her vehicle. The two said their goodbyes and she was on her way.

Chapter Two

"Hi, Megan. I'm pulling out of my garage. I should be there shortly." Damita's cell phone message went straight to voicemail.

Megan and Damita had made a date to attend Sunday morning serve at Tabernacle Baptist. As Terrell got up to deliver his 11:00 am sermon First Lady Damita straggled in late with Megan by her side distracting the congregation. Damita and Megan took adjacent seats front and center of the altar.

Terrell's message was taken from the Bible book of Genesis. It hit home with Damita. He preached that God promised Sarah and Abraham a son even though both were aged.

"The sermon is timely and appropriate," Damita took note.

"How is that so?" Megan asked still trying to listen to the message.

"Terrell and I was discussing infertility just the other night."

"Oh really."

"We've been trying to have a baby since the onset of our marriage."

Eddie Johnson

"Now that you have gotten that off your chest, hush woman, I'm trying to listen to the Word," Megan said playfully; yet she was serious.

The ladies fully refocused as Terrell went forth with his message. He put added emphasis on his words. "Tired of waiting Sarah had her husband Abraham sleep with Hagar a servant woman to conceive a child. The child was given the name Ishmael."

"A steamy love story in the Bible, I never knew that," Megan noted. "Whew." She swiftly waved a fan.

"And now you know. Attending church has never been your forte."

"Abraham ended up with two sons," Terrell eventually concluded his sermon. "Though Abraham fathered a son through Hagar a woman servant, God still made good on his promise to Abraham. Sarah his wife also bore a son they named Isaac. Sarah was age 90 at his birth."

"Maybe I'll join a church, when I'm done having fun," Megan responded to Damita's earlier comment.

Megan's Fools Paradise

Following the benediction, Damita met with Terrell briefly in his office.

Megan walked in after inadvertently being stopped because of a case of mistaken identity by Deacon Milford Whitfield.

"I would introduce you to Megan," Damita said. "But you and Megan have already met."

"Hi Terrell."

"Hi Megan. How are you?"

"I'm fine now. Your sermon was uplifting." She slyly smiled. "I'm definitely going to revisit. Who knows? I may become one of your members."

"You should join us tonight for dinner, we'll be entertaining my brother Daniel from Brooklyn."

"Yes Megan," Damita agreed. "You should join us."

"Say no more. Let me know the time and the restaurant. I'll meet you all there."

"I'll call you a little later after I drop you back home; once we settle on the cuisine, and the restaurant."

Terrell placed a short sweet kiss upon Damita's lips. The ladies departed Terrell's office.

Eddie Johnson

Megan checked with the reservationist at Jack Delano's Steakhouse.

"Hi Megan. I'm Tania your waitress. Your guest they are waiting. She handed Megan a menu. Right this way. I'll show you to their table." Tania promptly seated Megan and jotted down her order. She would provide her guest throughout their dinner the first-class service the five-star restaurant so prided themselves.

"Sorry, I'm late. I didn't expect the traffic to be so heavy," Megan apologized.

"You're fine," Terrell spoke. "We were late too. We only got here a few minutes ago. Meet my brother Danial."

"Hi. Megan. Your beauty precedes you. It's a pleasure to make your acquaintance."

"Hi Danial, "Megan sniggered. "I'm sure that's now how you'd normally greet a lady."

"Only when I'm being introduced to someone like yourself – a nice looking young lady."

The table went quiet for a moment.

"Terrell," Damita said. "Megan has agreed to volunteer at our now fully funded Irene Haywood Foundation's Domestic Violence Shelter.

Megan's Fools Paradise

Construction on the facility is set to start within the next few months." She looked towards Megan and then back to Terrell. "Megan should feel right at home assisting girls and women in need once it's finished."

"I never knew Megan to be that type..." Terrell stopped speaking.

"That's because you never knew my friend Megan before she stopped by our house and I wasn't available."

Terrell's mind temporarily reflected on the night mentioned. He vividly recalled the recent dinner shared with Megan as his house followed by a warm embraced and their kiss. He also briefly thought back to his past sexual involvement with Megan in Philadelphia.

"Were you listening? Hello! Terrell! You seem to be in deep thought."

"I'm sorry. You were saying something about not being available."

Megan looked to Danial. "How long are you planning on being in Atlanta," Megan queried. "You're nice and you are handsome. Two qualities I desire in a man."

Eddie Johnson

"Stop right there. Terrell's brother is already taken. Daniel is married, and he has three lovely kids; a daughter nine, and two boys ages five and seven. Believe me. You wouldn't want to tangle with his wife Krista."

"Danial. I didn't know. Please forgive me," Megan paused. "I should not have been so forward."

Aside from Terrell and Megan's miscues in communicating the dinner was a success.

Chapter Three

Several weeks went by from the time Damita and Megan were last together.

Damita knocked at Megan's apartment. "Hi. I was about to leave," Megan answered. "A guy I met the other night begged me for a date."

"I won't be long," Damita was quick to assure Megan.

"I have a few minutes. Come in. So, what's the reason for your visit?"

"The Irene Heywood foundation will meet Saturday afternoon. You previously express an interest in our organization. We're putting together a panel of speakers for an empowerment banquet to encourage young women to live up to their God given potentials. I was thinking perhaps you could be one of our panelist."

"I don't know. I'm just now beginning to grow, or should I say mature myself. I'll have to think about it." Megan finished putting on her earrings and then hurriedly strapped on her open toed stilettos.

Eddie Johnson

"You've already agreed to help out at the shelter. This should be an easy decision. Call me on Friday night."

"I'll be sure to let you know then. Okay."

"Sounds fair enough."

Megan changed the discussion. "I have good news to share."

"Ooh girl. Don't tell me. Let me guess. You got the history professor position."

"Yes! During my last interview I was cross examined by three top ranking seasoned professors. I knocked the ball out of the park! I'm officially on Staff!"

"I suppose you'll be starting in a couple of weeks when the summer session commences."

"Damita! I got hired just in the nick of time! Your home-girl Megan was on the verge of being evicted. My landlord was about to serve me notice."

"Well Megan, I won't hold you any longer. You have a date with a young man."

"Claude isn't young. He's somewhat older. You are right; however, I shouldn't keep him waiting. If I leave now, we'll meet at our agreed upon time."

Megan's Fools Paradise

"I have something of yours. I found it in the hallway that intersects with my family room and kitchen."

"You found something of mine!" Megan exclaimed. "What did I leave behind?"

Damita reached down into her handbag. "Your makeup kit…" She handed it to Megan. "I've been toting it around ever since the morning after my domestic violence luncheon."

"One last question before you leave. How is Daniel? Is he still in town?"

"Megan. Are you okay. I never knew you to be into married men. I told you, Daniel is not available."

"I was just making conversation. No pun or harm intended."

Saturday afternoon, Damita pulled into the parking lot of the Irene Heywood Foundation. She drove past Megan sitting patiently in her vehicle.

Damita and Megan met up at the front entrance to the facility.

Eddie Johnson

"I'm sorry, I didn't call. Last night I was still undecided about your panelist offer. I decided at the last minute to meet you here this afternoon."

During the foundation's meeting Megan officially became a member of the organization. Megan wasted no time in putting her best foot forward as to why should be allowed on the empowerment panel.

"I offer a motion to accept Megan Hightower to the aforementioned mentor task," Victoria Stallworth asserted.

"And I second the motion," Damita articulated.

"Let everyone in agreement let it be known by a show of hands!" Chairman Brooke Dunsford shouted. "It's a unanimous decision. Ms. Megan, you have been confirmed!"

Chapter Four

Tabernacle Baptist Church's Sisters Anita Tillman and Joyce Knowles chatted in the vestibule of the sanctuary prior to early Sunday morning service.

Joyce relished spreading gossip. "Rumor has it that our beloved Minister Terrell Crutchfield is cheating on our First Lady."

"Hopefully it's just that Ms. Joyce a rumor," Anita hesitated and then followed. "That's the reason Tabernacle Baptist's last minister was let go."

"When confronted with the infidelity accusation by my anonymous source Minister Crutchfield termed the allegation as baseless nonsense which should not be repeated."

"Please enlighten me," Anita said.

"Supposedly, Minister Crutchfield has been slipping around with Madeline Webster," Joyce spoke forth. "She's a new member of our congregation."

"How could our minister stoop so low?" Anita wondered aloud.

Eddie Johnson

Anita was bound to spill the beans sooner or later to her friend Damita about her husband's alleged adulterous affair.

Sunday morning service proceeded as usual for Minister Crutchfield until he opened the doors to the church.

Megan answered the altar call for membership. "Excuse me, Damita," Megan spoke as she squeezed by exiting their pew. Damita smiled. Megan gently glided into the friendly welcoming embrace of Damita's husband.

Damita thought to herself: *I trust my friend Megan is joining the church for the right reason; which would be to give her life over to Christ, and not because my husband Terrell is the senior minister.*

Following the benediction Damita and Megan headed towards the nearest exit.

Anita walked past them. "Hi girls. I'm in a hurry." She spoke in passing. "Damita. We need to talk. Give me a call."

Chapter Five

Ferdinand Jean University's summer term was in full swing as Megan effortlessly transitioned into her role as a history professor.

Megan's ambitious joyous achievement would be short lived. The news media broke fresh news of accreditation and budgetary problems plaguing Ferdinand Jean University.

Damita, Megan, and Anita met at Antonio Giovanni's Italian Pub and Restaurant to celebrate Megan's latest career move. Their weekend night out was to provide Megan a much-needed release from a grueling yet rewarding week.

During dinner Damita posed an indirect question. "Anita. Several weeks ago, on your way out of church you said that I should give you a holler."

"Yes. I have something to tell you. But now is not a good time." She paused. "It's about your husband Derrick."

Megan got the cue. "Excuse me girls, I'm going to visit the ladies room. I need to refresh."

Damita and Anita waited for Megan to leave.

Eddie Johnson

"I'm going to tell you," Anita proceeded. "A rumor has been circulating at church that your beloved husband our minister has been and continues to be unfaithful to you."

"That explains the talk behind my back by the holier than thou women at church."

"You probably don't believe them."

"Why should I believe unsubstantiated rhetoric? Some of them would die to trade places with me."

"My anonymous source is quite reliable."

"Oh! Spare me the details!"

"No. You should know. I said rumor. But I believe it. Your husband was observed with Madeline Webster. The floozy was all up in Terrell's face at an out of town night club."

"Is that all you have to tell?" Damita asked.

"No. There is more. My source further stated the twosome has been spotted at various discreet locations around our fair city."

"Who is Madeline Webster?"

"I doubt you know Madeline. She's relatively new to our congregation."

*M*egan's *F*ools *P*aradise

"I'm going to give Terrell the benefit of the doubt. I trust him. I will not allow you or anyone to come between us."

"Fine Damita. Go ahead. Believe what you want about your deceitful husband."

Damita sat quietly. She didn't utter another word until Megan returned.

"Ladies the night is getting old," Megan said. "You both have been great. Thank you."

As they were leaving the restaurant Megan took a moment to chat with Damita.

"Are you okay? Unlike when we started tonight you now appear distraught."

"I'm just a little perturbed. But fine. According to Anita, Terrell is cheating."

"We both know that's not true. Terrell wouldn't do anything to ever hurt you."

"I know. I trust Terrell."

Chapter Six

Megan was feeling low. She dialed Damita's cell phone. Damita promptly answered.

"Last weekend we celebrated my coming aboard at the university," Megan ranted.

"And that was good," Damita said.

"Today things have changed," Megan further conveyed. "I switched on the television when I arrived home and the university seem to be in an upheaval."

"What are you saying?"

"According to the evening news our Ferdinand Jean University has accreditation and budgetary issues. The university has now two failed attempts to meet accreditation guidelines. You must have known about the first failed attempt."

"I did know. I thought; however, everything had been resolved."

"Unfortunately, it hasn't! And now I'm in a damn predicament!"

"Try to remain calm. Everything will be fine."

"I can't. I must get this out of my system. Funding for the university has been cut and the administrators has no choice but to layoff personnel." Megan cleared her throat.

"That really hits home. The Lord will see us through. I'm going to lift up our university and us in prayer."

"Perhaps the Lord will help you. I don't believe I'm on His list to be blessed. I'm one of the last hired and I will be among the first to be let go. The university's budgetary woes will only worsen. The University cannot accept any new students until they've been fully accredited."

"I know things seem bad," Damita said. "Are they really that dire?"

"If I'm laid off. And I will be laid off from work. If I pay my rent. I will not have enough funds to survive. My only options are welfare or getting a sugar daddy or two to support me."

"I'm going to talk with Terrell. I cannot have my best friend being thrown out onto the streets. I don't envision you being a hustler."

"I have done it. While in Miami I fell on hard times. I serviced a few Johns on the streets. I had a very demanding pimp."

"Why not ask your parents for help?"

Eddie Johnson

"My mother got pregnant just when she thought her child bearing days were over. Mom and the baby died during the delivery. That happened right before I left to start college in Florida."

"I'm sorry Megan. I didn't mean to be insensitive."

"And you probably would like to know about my father too. I suppose. After mom passed away my father had a lifestyle change. He underwent an operation. I found out that he is gay."

"Your father is transgender."

"Yes. And we haven't spoken since. My father Aaron changed his legal name to Erica."

"Tabernacle Baptist would be the obvious place for you to look for help in a crisis."

"I should seek assistance from my church home. That's what you are suggesting. Am I right?"

"No. That's not what I am saying."

"And why wouldn't it be in my case? Is it because I'm still new to Tabernacle Baptist?"

"The church has over extended itself in debt. Our church treasure is low." She paused. "But don't you worry, Megan. I'm going to ask your minister-my husband to allow you to move in with

*M*egan's *F*ools *P*aradise

us. If it's alright with Terrell, your problem is solved. Let's change the subject."

"To what?" Megan asked.

"We should talk about the upcoming women's empowerment conference. I know you've prepared to speak. Saturday will be the big day."

"Taking in account my soon to be financial trouble and my stint in Miami as a hooker, I should withdraw from The Irene Heywood Foundation's squeaky-clean panel."

"Megan. I bet you none of the women on the panel are without blemish. You should relax. You have nothing to fear. Hard times only makes people like you stronger."

"Perhaps you're right. I'm going to suck up my personal woes for a day, so I can help others."

"Amen Sister Megan."

Chapter Seven

The Irene Haywood Foundation's Women Conference and Luncheon went on as scheduled in the banquet Hall of the Peach Center Inn. Megan Hightower was the last speaker to grace the podium whose penchant was to note the importance of a good education.

A young adult woman participating in the question and answer period following the panelist presentations made a personal reference and inquiry to Megan. "It's been all over the local news lately," she asserted and paused. "Ferdinand Jean University will be laying off personnel due to budget cuts. You stated that you're a newly hired professor at Ferdinand Jean University. Aren't you the least bit concerned that your job could be in endanger of being cut?"

"I'll answer your question but not from a personal perspective. That not the intent of this platform. I believe, however, by taking advantage of career and/or job training initiatives one should be able to set aside funds to get them through trying times. One should also keep close at hand family and friends who are capable of providing moral and financial support."

Following the empowerment conference and luncheon the attendees were treated to a job fair plus a myriad of help sessions presented by local support groups.

Ferdinand Jeans University's summer term ended. Management handed pink slips to staff with the least tenure. Megan's eyes flooded with tears as she accepted her anticipated dreaded layoff notice.

Strapped from struggling to put herself through college Megan was at the mercy of the Lord.

Megan paid a penalty to her landlord, so she could be relieved of her rental agreement. She then secured her non-essential possessions in public storage.

Damita and Terrell welcomed Megan into their home to stay if needed until she could get back on her feet.

"You guys are wonderful. If it's the Lord will one day I will repay you."

Eddie Johnson

"As your minister I will not hear it," Terrell vowed. "It's my God given duty and right to see my members through dark times."

"Well Megan I can't top Terrell. Damita wiped tears from Megan's face. Heed my words of encouragement. Keep the faith. Hold your head high. We're in this together. Who knows? I may be let go in the next round of rumored layoffs."

"Tenure must mean something," Megan queried. "Don't you think?"

"The term tenured instructor at our university is loosely defined considering it's still in its infancy."

"At least you have a strong black well-educated man to cover your back."

"I concur-without a doubt," Damita noted.

Megan's eyes drifted towards Terrell. He smiled.

"Hand your luggage to Terrell. We'll show you to your bedroom."

Chapter Eight

Megan hungered for Terrell's embrace and for the sexual innuendoes he had been known to whisper.

Restless and unable to sleep Terrell arose early with a few hours to spare before his part time police officer shift was to begin. Damita had minutes ago departed for work at the university still oblivious to the fact of Megan and her husband's past and present involvement.

Running watered lured Terrell to check out its source. He opened the door to the guest bathroom. Megan took notice of the patter of Terrell's familiar footsteps. Through the steamed-up glass shower enclosure shown a darkened silhouette. Megan's hands slipped from the shower door as it hurled backwards. Megan's bare physique covered in sweltering moistness drew Terrell who quickly disrobed. Like magnets Terrell and Megan were fused in the shower caught up in the heat of passion. The lust driven sexual activity which carried over into Megan's guest bedroom lasted until Terrell forced himself to ready for work.

Eddie Johnson

Damita acknowledged Megan as she arrived home in the afternoon. "So. How was your day? Hopefully it was better than mine."

"It was a fairly productive day, "Megan replied. "It started out great. And then it took a downward spiral. I handed out my killer resume to select local colleges and universities which didn't require its submittal online. My only hope at present appears to be Seth College. It's comparable to Ferdinand Jean University but on a smaller scale. I interviewed there today."

"How much smaller?" Damita asked.

"You shouldn't ask. You don't want to know."

"It can't be that bad."

"Well. Seth College is located within a shopping center. It occupies several adjoining storefronts. I should know in a few weeks if they're interested. Their medical and financial benefits package offered would start from day one."

"It sounds interesting; however, you should think it thoroughly through. Similar colleges have turned out to be diploma mills with their own financial gain their major objective."

*M*egan's *F*ools *P*aradise

"Perhaps you are right. But if I should get hired I'll take my chances."

"It's your call." Damita shifted topics. "I too have good news to report."

"Really."

"Yes. Because of The Irene Heywood Foundation's Conference and Luncheon, we have now been granted television and radio spots to explain our outreach program in detail to our whole community."

"Megan smiled. "That is great news."

"And you were a part of it," Damita acknowledged. "You were a smash."

Terrell and Megan started looking more and more to their early morning sexual escapades. Damita should have been suspicious of their sneaking. Whenever Terrell's name was brought up Megan's physical demeanor changed and she sheepishly avoided eye contact.

"Hi Damita. What a timing coincidence. I was just about to call you," Alana Wooten acknowledged and greeted her daughter over her cell phone."

"Hi mom."

"How are things going in Atlanta?" Alana queried. "I can hardly wait for next month to visit you and my minister son in law."

"We are fine. Thank the Lord."

"You say that you are fine. But I hear discontent in your voice."

"I know. The university is having funding issues. Its future is shaky."

"I thank God every day for our fortune your father and I amassed in the stock market. You father and I made sure of your financial stability by sharing our wealth. You shouldn't worry."

"You couldn't be righter. However, it's not about money. I enjoy working with the students at Ferdinand Jean University."

"I'm sure you do. We'll trust the Lord to intercede into the university's business affairs so that they're able to rebound bountifully."

"You're right mom. We've always been blessed. The Lord has always provided us with a covering."

Megan's Fools Paradise

"If I had my way I would move back to Atlanta. Your father Bill on the other hand loves New York City."

"Maybe you will too. Give it time. The Big Apple probably needs time to grow on you."

"I don't see that ever happening. I will never-ever pry him away from New York even with a crowbar."

"Enough said about New York." Damita hesitated. "When you arrive to find another woman in the house, I don't want you to be startled by her presence. I and Terrell have taken in a friend. She'll be staying with us until she gets back up on her feet."

"It's not every day a married woman invites another woman into their home."

"You're right mom. But she's not just anybody. Megan Hightower is my old best friend from high school."

"She is Vera Hightower's daughter. I remember Megan. I can sum her up in two words boy – struck. Megan flirted with any Tom, Dick or Harry which crossed her path."

Eddie Johnson

"I know Mom. Megan was a harmless flirt. And she's matured. You'll see for yourself."

Chapter Nine

Terrell glued to a late-night cable sports cast failed to notice Damita when she trailed off to their bedroom. Before hitting the sack, Damita listened to her cell phone's voice mail. The last message played was the kicker. *"You are such a fool. Your husband is under investigation by our church Deacon Board. Be forewarned by my alert. The woman staying under your roof should not be trusted."* The audio stopped. She couldn't place the soft-spoken female's voice.

Cletus Brunson the church's outspoken Chairman of the Deacon Board called a special meeting the following evening.

"We now have sufficient evidence to move forward with a recall." The chairman jeered gloatingly. "I have a written revelation from a female member which brings to light appalling immoral behavior by our minister."

"We never envisioned Minister Crutchfield as our church leader," Deacon Cedrick Spikes added spitefully. "Am I right my Godly brothers?" Some of the guys nodded in agreement while others verbally agreed."

"Take note." The chairman circulated a written account he referenced. "Madeline Webster; our source, was a past lover of Minister Crutchfield who she claimed jilted her prior to being converted over to the Lord. After joining Tabernacle Baptist, the two were subsequently reunited. Women from the church witnessed them slipping around in the city although they were trying to be discreet. A couple of the women convinced Madeline to break off their callous ungodly relationship and to testify along with them against Minister Crutchfield."

"Sounds to me that Ms. Madeline had it in for Minister Crutchfield; since he rejected, or should I say ditched her in a past relationship."

"It doesn't matter," Deacon Brunson added. "A man of the Lord should have known better. The graphic love undertakings between them which Madeline depicted cannot be ignored."

"The man is crazy. He has a fine to eye, well-educated intellectual wife; yet he is stupid enough to commit adultery."

Megan's Fools Paradise

"Tone it down Deacon Johnson; until he's recalled the man is still the head of our church."

A recall committee consisting of the head of each ministry was unanimously approved by vote.

Deacon Horace Solomon prayed, and the meeting was adjourned.

Chapter Ten

"I would like to come clean! Allow me to apologize at least; so, we can move on with our inevitable future!" Megan fumed as she climbed the spiraled staircase toward Damita standing on the second-floor landing.

"How could you!" Damita's voice loudly echoed throughout the vast open enclosure. "Megan! You betrayed me under my own roof! You slept with my man!"

"I know Terrell informed you of my pregnancy." Megan stopped dead in her tracks. "This isn't going to sound right. We should have been more open in our communication."

"Damn right!" Damita shouted.

"And if we had this tragedy wouldn't have ever taken place. We should have told you…"

"Told me what? Bitch! Finish your statement!"

"Terrell and I were involved romantically when we graduated high school. It was a brief fling."

"So, you think words can justify you being impregnated by a woman's husband!"

Megan threw up her hands as she attempted to put a foot on the next step; but she fell backwards instead, and plummeted down the dimly lit narrowed stairway.

Damita summoned paramedics who upon arrival found Megan sprawled at the foot of the stairs. Megan's pulse was faint, and she was unconscious.

Terrell came home; hastily, he parked in front of the house. Exiting his vehicle Terrell witnessed paramedics as they pushed through his front door wheeling a stretcher carrying Megan to an awaiting emergency transport ambulance.

Terrell yelled to Damita seeking an explanation. "Damita! What in the hell happened? What did you do?"

"I didn't do anything. We were talking. Megan fell down the stairs."

"I don't believe you! Why didn't you let me handle it?"

"Megan came home in a rage. She wanted talk. I wasn't in the mood. So, I headed upstairs on the way to our bedroom. I stopped after reaching the top of the stairs. We got into a heated verbal exchange. Somehow Megan lost her footing. She tumbled."

Eddie Johnson

Terrell got back into his vehicle. He drove around aimlessly. His initial intent was to check on Megan at the hospital. Selfishly the distraught minister concluded that the child could not have possibly survived Megan's traumatic plunge. On the outskirts of the city stressed to the point of nearly cracking Terrell almost steered his car into a massive retention pond. Avoiding a watery grave, Terrell headed back to his house to try in salvaging his distressed marriage. As Terrell approached the house, Damita backed her vehicle out of their driveway. She stopped next to him.

"I didn't expect you to be back so soon. I'm on my way to break the bad news to Erica."

"Who's Erica?"

"Megan's father Aaron. He's now Erica." She drove away.

Terrell shook his head. He thought to himself *Damita didn't ask about Megan nor the baby. She doesn't know just like I don't know if they are dead or alive.*

Chapter Eleven

"You're Megan's first visitor." The front desk clerk at Medford Medical Center informed Erica.

"That's odd. According to a friend of Megan, she should have received another visitor."

"Only family and clergy of patients in the Intensive Care Unit can visit."

"Minister Terrell Crutchfield of Tabernacle Baptist Church left earlier this afternoon enroute to the hospital to visit with Megan."

"I'm sure the good minister if asked will account for his absence. Sign here. You're first on the list."

Stopping at the hospital's ICU desk, Nurse Tisdale greeted Erica. "I'll need to prepare you to enter the germ-free environment of Megan's room. But first you'll need a briefing." She gestured towards a middle age woman approaching the nurse's station.

"You must be Erica Hightower."

"Yes. And who are you?"

"I'm Doctor Beverly Davis, your daughter Megan's doctor."

"How is my daughter and the baby?"

Eddie Johnson

"Your daughter is a warrior. She's fighting for her life."

Erica waited for the doctor to finish speaking. She didn't.

"You didn't mention the baby."

Dr. Davis looked Megan straight in the eyes. "I'm sorry. Your daughter is the sole survivor."

Nurse Tisdale prepared Erica for her daughter's isolation room visit. In the darkened ICU room Erica fought back her tears as she observed Megan heavily sedated being feed intravenously.

Sunday morning, First Lady Damita failed to show up for church. Terrell preached as hard as he could but the Holy Ghost fire that normally took a hold of the congregation could not be lit.

Following the benediction, Deacon Board Chairman Cletus Brunson flagged down the minister in the hallway. "Minister Crutchfield, may I accompany you to your office. We should talk."

"Sure Deacon. My door is always open."

In the office Deacon Brunson spoke. "How is Damita or should I say Mrs. Crutchfield."

*M*egan's *F*ools *P*aradise

"Damita decided to stay home. She wasn't feeling well."

"I hope she feels better."

"You have something else on your mind other than my wife. How may I help you deacon? Talk! I'm listening!"

"Deacon Tidwell tried visiting with Sister Megan Hightower. Megan is one of our new members assigned to his ward. According to him she moved. Correct me if I am wrong. Megan is living under the same roof as you and your wife."

"Megan experienced a financial setback. She's a friend of Damita. We welcomed her into our home."

"The arrangement you referenced seemed fine until a young lady stopped me in the church's parking lot this morning. She said the relationship between you, Megan, and your wife Damita was anything but wholesome."

"How could anyone possibly know what has been going on inside my house. The buzzards are circling. Their intent is to destroy me. Lord grant me strength."

Eddie Johnson

"Minister Crutchfield. I hope the allegation is false. It should be noted that my findings both from Deacon Tidwell and the anonymous female this morning will be reported to the Deacon Board. Your popularity in the church is waning."

Chapter Twelve

Damita with iPod earbuds firmly inserted, and gospel music popping was ready for an early Saturday morning jog. A Silverado pickup truck whirled into the house's driveway as she locked up the front door. She focused in on the driver. It was Erica.

"Hi Damita. I hate to trouble you. But I need to get Megan's belongings. The hospital will be releasing Megan tomorrow. She's going to be staying with me. I appreciate what you've done up until now for my daughter."

"So how is the baby?" Damita asked.

"Regrettably the baby didn't survive the incident."

"Oh no. I should have known."

"And that's a real shame," Erica frankly noted. She then reiterated. "It's a real shame. You would have known if your husband a poor excuse for a minister had not neglected to check on Megan at the hospital."

"I'm sorry for your loss. You and Megan must be devastated. Please accept my apology for my husband's unorthodox behavior."

Eddie Johnson

"Alright sugar. You're forgiven. He was so wrong. I was just telling my friend-girl the other day about your self-centered uncaring husband. Debra said there isn't anything Godly about a whore-monger. My dear friend is seriously thinking about moving her tabernacle Baptist membership."

"Okay, Erica enough about my man. Follow me inside. I already have Ms. Megan's bags packed."

During the succeeding week Sasha Rutgers, a social worker with the Georgia Family Services Department met with Terrell at work and then with Damita at their home. Sasha's GFSD investigation was to find or rule out possible motives for any criminal activity which could have led to Megan's fall.

The Deacon Board was briefed by Paula Dees the overseer of the recall committee. "Two harlots of our church Madeline Webster and Megan Hightower both hold keys for us to secure a successful recall."

"Mrs. Dees please refrain from name calling." The Deacon Board Chairman demanded.

Megan's Fools Paradise

"That's fine. Deacon Brunson. I'll try to be more selective if need be of my characterizations. Gentlemen as you're aware Minister Crutchfield jilted Ms. Webster during a past relationship and that Minister Crutchfield since ditched Ms. Webster again after she joined Tabernacle Baptist. You have her written acknowledgement of those facts."

"And what do you have to add?" Deacon Whitfield questioned.

"Ms. Madeline flabbergasted and taken aback by all the hoopla which has arisen has provided our recall committee a complete verbal bares all account of their sordid affairs which includes video footage plus photos." Mrs. Dees looked around to gage reactions.

"Keep talking Mrs. Dees," instructed the chairman.

"The account included her own personalized journaled times, dates and places of unholy forbidden acts undertaken before and after she hooked up with Tabernacle Baptist."

"We need for you to share the details," Deacon Spikes urged.

Eddie Johnson

"The first relationship was a swinger, or you could say an open sexual association."

"Define open sexual association?" Deacon Johnson sought clarity.

"Megan and our minister in their past engaged in simultaneous sexual intercourse with multiple partners on several occasions. When she tried to close the involvement just to themselves Minister Crutchfield walked."

"The woman has no shame!" Deacon Whitfield blurted.

"She is cold-blooded without a doubt," Deacon Spikes vindictively roared. "It's definitely a case of sweet adulterated revenge!"

"Brace yourself gentlemen," Ms. Dees scoffed. "You all know Sister Debra Lovejoy. Well. She's revealed an even more alarming sexual fiasco which involved yet another woman and our Minister Crutchfield."

"Not another woman! He's undoubtedly out of his mind!"

The room went quiet. "I'll tell it the way Ms. Lovejoy thoroughly enlightened me. Megan Hightower a longtime friend of our First Lady

*M*egan's *F*ools *P*aradise

Damita recently got laid off from work. Minister Crutchfield and the first Lady felt sorry for Megan. So, they invited Damita's friend Megan into their home."

"What was our First Lady thinking?" Deacon Spikes thought allowed.

"I agree. But let me finish."

"Okay."

"The agreement was that Megan would live with our First Family until she could recover financially. It seemed to be the right thing to do. Within the walls of Minister Crutchfield's supposedly sanctimonious home he and Ms. Megan started having sex. Megan got pregnant."

Sounds of disbelief from those in attendance reverberated throughout the room.

Mrs. Dees went forth with her report. "When Damita found out that Megan was expecting a baby by her husband – a heated argument ensued between Damita and her friend. Megan's concentration was lost as she misstepped climbing the dwelling's spiraled stairway. She tumbled to the foot of the stairs. Megan was rushed to the nearest hospital. And not once while Megan was

Eddie Johnson

hospitalized did Minister Crutchfield pay a visit. She miscarried the baby."

"The man has no scruples or conscious," Deacon Whitfield yelled. "He shouldn't be a Minister! He has to go!"

Chapter Thirteen

Terrell engaged in an intense talk with Damita right as he arrived home from work. "I plan to travel out to California next week."

"You probably need to clear your head," Damita added. "I understand. We have been challenged a lot lately."

"Damita. My concern goes beyond what you are thinking. And Proactively I have developed a plan to address my future. I have an interview scheduled for a full-time police officer position in Los Angeles."

"Why Los Angeles. Why not seek a full time correctional facility or police department position locally?"

"Some disenchanted members of my church's congregation are plotting against me. I would hate to have to deal with the humility of living locally if I'm forced out as their minister."

"Without further ado I think you should rethink your decision."

"That's an ultimatum I will not accept."

"And I refuse to move away with a man who I can't trust in pursuit of a restructured life for him to hide or forget a shameful past. If you mess up your bed you should prepare to sleep in it."

The next morning at the Hightower's house Erica and Megan would chat over breakfast. Erica had made Megan's favorite blue berry muffin pancakes.

"I should slit my wrist and be done with you and everyone! What good is my life?" Megan cried out.

"Dear. Please. Don't go there." Erica pleaded with Megan.

"Why not? I lost my mother during a midlife child bearing effort and to boot I lost my father Aaron who now revels in trans-sexuality."

"I still love you-Megan, whether you accept me as who I am or not. Don't give up on life. You have family members who care deeply for you. If you need psychotherapy, I'll arrange for it."

"I betrayed my best friend." Megan seethed. "I wake up at night sometimes in a cold sweat crying from dreaming about my baby I miscarried. I probably have destroyed Terrell's marriage and church ministry."

"Sugar. Terrell doesn't deserve your sympathy."

Megan's Fools Paradise

"I got a rude awakening at church last night during bible study. I went looking for comfort. A young female referred to me as a homewrecker and a baby killer."

"I don't believe it." Erica turned away. She dropped her head.

"Someone had leaked my recent involvement with Minister Crutchfield and that I'd been pregnant with his child."

"I-only-told-Debra," Erica slowly murmured. "I thought Debra could be trusted."

Chapter Fourteen

Minister Crutchfield propelled his sports utility vehicle a black Lincoln MKX into Tabernacle Baptist's less than half capacity filled parking lot. He had anticipated an even worse turn out.

Humiliated beyond belief he walked swiftly into the sanctuary's side entrance with his briefcase in hand and head held high.

His first sermon of the morning was delivered without incident.

First Lady Damita was still absent.

Minister Crutchfield who had been known for mingling with his parishioners hid out in his office between services.

A ruckus would slightly delay the beginning of the second service.

Sitting incognito sporting a large brim hat on a back pew was Megan Hightower. Even though disguised beneath the walloping head accessory Minister Crutchfield was still able to identify Megan.

Two ghetto young women from a neighboring hood name Lolita and Corliss approached Megan.

*M*egan's *F*ools *P*aradise

"You need to get up – and you need to leave!" Lolita put an arm around Megan's Shoulders."

"Don't cause no trouble – and there want be none!" Corliss quickly added.

Megan Lunged upward with her hand outstretched. She forcibly pushed the young woman who had groped her shoulders into an unoccupied adjacent space.

Rushing from their assigned posts ushers took hold of the two trouble makers. Megan with pocketbook swinging bolted out of the sanctuary. As Megan was leaving up walked Damita for the first time in several weeks. Their eyes met. They exchanged cutting glances.

"Get out of my way!" Megan bellowed.

Sensing Megan's discomfort, Damita joked. "Megan. You act like you met up with a ghost inside."

"Whew," she fumed. "I do not have time for your melodrama! Step aside. You're blocking my path!"

In the wee hours of the night two battered souls wrestled with their own future ideologies.

Eddie Johnson

An anguished Terrell packed his bags for an early morning flight to Los Angeles.

Damita spoke with tears in eyes. "I should not have been so foolish. I should not have tempted you by allowing Megan to move in with us."

"You weren't aware of our past involvement. It wasn't your fault."

"I know. I was friend to someone I should have never trusted."

Terrell's words faltered as his mind fast forwarded. "I'm going to find a job in California; rest assured, even if it isn't one of two I'll interview for over the next three days."

"Terrell, I was hoping you would reconsider moving. But…"

"I haven't changed my stance on relocating!" Terrell blurted after interrupting. "And I doubt you've changed yours!"

"You don't…"

"I did not think so!" He again cut her off. "You remain dead set against it!"

"Actually, I had given it some thought. I was thinking of joining you in Los Angeles. Although at this time, I'm again leaning towards staying put.

Megan's Fools Paradise

Terrell Crutchfield, maybe you should go your own way. I'm tired of your petty disregard and disrespect!

Chapter Fifteen

Daisy Allison the church secretary listened to what she perceived was a perplexing voice message left by Minister Crutchfield. She rationalized it was out of character for a senior pastor to leave his home base without notice. It started off saying he was on his way flying to Los Angeles for three days to relax and to meet with Minister Travis Boatwright a former classmate from Harvey Ellis Christian Seminary.

Deacon Board Chairman Brunson walked in as Daisy was locking up the church's office. She had concluded her work day.

"Deacon Brunson. How are you?"

"I am fine. How are you Daisy?"

"I'm good. My work day is finally done."

"I received your text and voice mail advising me of Minister Crutchfield's sudden urge to venture out to California. I and my deacons will have the incident investigated. It's not the first. We have had other recent notable situations checked out involving our besieged minister."

Megan's Fools Paradise

"That perhaps explains everything." Daisy appeared suddenly enlightened.

"What do you mean?"

"He's probably planning his exit. Sinful mess has hit the fan. He's seeing red. That's what I think."

Deacon Brunson chuckled. "I hate to run but I have to prepare to conduct tonight's bible study."

"Okay deacon. Take care. I'm headed home."

Megan received by way of mail a final interview invitation from Seth College. A full month had crept by since her first interview. She had all but given up on finding full time post-secondary education employment. The notification brought a long overdue ray of hope.

"At last I'm in contention for a college level professor position."

"I'm happy!" Erica exclaimed. "I knew it would only be a matter of time. When is your big interview?"

Megan beamed. "It's next Wednesday."

"I'm going to send up a special prayer."

Eddie Johnson

"Mother-Erica. Thank you. I'm sure the Lord will hear it."

"On that note, you need a new church home," Erica thought provokingly replied."

"You are right. I should move on. My last visit to Tabernacle Baptist was a wakeup call. I have already asked the Lord for his forgiveness."

Erica embraced Megan. "Maybe we'll find a church home that we can both share."

Meanwhile at the Crutchfield's house Damita was suddenly overcome by an unexpected anxiety attack as she spoke with her mom on the phone "Now is not a good time. You and dad should delay your visit to Atlanta."

"Why babe," Alana stated. "We've been waiting in anticipation for this visit too long. What could possibly warrant a postponement?"

"All hell has broken loose. My marriage is in shambles and Terrell is about to be kicked out as minister of his church."

"What happened?"

"That bombshell you warned me about. Well. Let's just say she and another exploded."

Megan's Fools Paradise

"You're talking about Vera's girl Megan and now some other woman too. I knew Megan couldn't be trusted."

"Don't rub it in mom, I had to find out the hard way. I hate to admit it. You were right about Megan. She is one of two floozies which Terrell appallingly cheated on me with from his past. His days at Tabernacle Baptist are numbered."

"I'm not sure how your overly protective father is going to react once I break the news. Bill still thinks of you as his baby."

"I just hope dad doesn't hop a plane here from New York to beat the crap out of Terrell."

"Bill has gotten older. Let's hope he has mellowed."

They laughed.

Chapter Sixteen

Terrell flew back from California ready to feel the raft of his church.

First on the minister's agenda was a meeting called by the Deacon Board to notify him of an upcoming vote on his ouster. Minister Crutchfield showed up to the meeting with his resignation letter in hand.

"We will hold on to your letter," Deacon Johnson the church treasurer made clear. "We figured you'd want to resign so that you could still claim your severance."

"It isn't that simple," Deacon Brunson said.

"Why can't it be that simple?"

"It's not your call," he replied. "The church will decide. They'll officially vote to accept your resignation or whether to give you the boot. A recall notification meeting letter has been mailed out to all our active members."

"Like it or not – it's only fitting," Deacon Morrison added. "Tabernacle Baptist should have the final say."

Megan's Fools Paradise

"If I'm not banned, gentlemen, I would love to preach my last sermon and to give a farewell message to the congregation on Sunday."

"We have no intention of blocking you from speaking on Sunday. You're still the minister. At least for now."

The brief informative meeting concluded.

Minister Crutchfield sat along in his office solemnly communing with God. He cried out for heavenly forgiveness and guidance. The Deacon Board meeting had left him mentally depleted.

Terrell spoke a verbal command into his cell phone. It dialed a number.

"Hello. Megan speaking." She recognized the name on the caller I.D. "Terrell! Why are you calling?"

"Hear me out," he pleaded.

"You have thirty seconds."

"I'm sorry I wasn't there for you and our baby at the hospital. I ask for your forgiveness. I would like to do right by you going forth."

"Stop! Why should I forgive you? You're feeling sorry isn't going to help my situation."

Eddie Johnson

"At least allow me to pay for your medical bills."

"That would be fine. I'll gladly let you take care of the medical bills. You are still, however, a sorry excuse for a man. You still haven't acknowledged to me the death of our child."

"In my mind I'm still grappling with the reality of it all. A part of me died."

"The baby – fetal remains were cremated," Megan voiced cracked. Tears flooded her eyes." A funeral chaplain at a local mortuary performed a passing ceremony."

"You're right. I should have been there. Although I know your relatives in attendance they would not have approved." He hesitated. "Forward your medical bills to my home address. Damita will make sure I get them."

Megan's sobbing escalated. The phone connection dropped.

Chapter Seventeen

Minister Crutchfield rendered his final Sunday morning sermon at Tabernacle Baptist. Another lackluster number of parishioners were on hand.

The carefully groomed message was about King David of Jerusalem in the Bible who impregnated a woman named Bathsheba. The king had lustfully observed as she bathed from the roof of his palace. He later sent her husband to war into a battle in which he was killed. Yet King David remained a man after God's own heart.

After Minster Crutchfield awkwardly compared himself to King David he then transitioned from his message into his farewell. "I'm sorry for such short notice. This will be my last Sunday here at Tabernacle Baptist. I have submitted my resignation." He touched on his accomplishments; emphasizing the most notable, since his inception, their improved mission's department.

One lone troubled member of the congregation waited until the end of service to spoil their minister's otherwise flawless exit. A woman asked for and was promptly granted permission by Minister Crutchfield to give a testimony. As she

Eddie Johnson

strutted down the center isle breezing past the
First Lady it dawned on him that the woman was
none other than Madeline Webster.

"Hear Me!" Madeline Shouted. "I have a
conscious! I will not sit idly by without presenting
the other sordid side of your minister. I'll be as
brief as possible. Minister Crutchfield has always
been a womanizer. He jilted me twice; once before
and after I became a member of his flock."

The members became restless. The noise level
grew.

"Yeah. You heard me! Minister Crutchfield had
an affair with me! He committed adultery! If that
wasn't a bad enough act Minister Crutchfield then
slept with his wife's best friend; one of our new
members, a Ms. Megan Hightower."

The noise level in the sanctuary got even louder
once Madeline released the verbal bomb shell.
"Megan got impregnated by Minister Crutchfield.
She fell down the stairs at his house. The baby
was lost. I personally believe the first lady sitting
there on the front pew assisted in the fall. That
would make our First Lady-Damita a murderer."

Megan's Fools Paradise

Enraged by being falsely labeled a murderer Damita rushed towards Madeline. Ushers quickly grabbed the women and pulled them apart before their flaying fists connected. Minister Crutchfield sprinted from the pulpit and stood in the gap. He adjourned church without giving the benediction.

Chapter Eighteen

"Last night Tabernacle Baptist rendered their recall decision," Terrell noted. "Today I'm the talk of the city. Every local news media outlet whether television, radio, print, or online depicts me as a disgraced minister of a mega church thrown out by his parishioners by an almost unanimous vote."

Terrell had a completely made up mind. There would be no leeway for negotiation.

Damita and Terrell as of late sat around their dining room table in somewhat of a dire somber mood. Damita had prepared one of his favorite dishes.

"I'd be disappointed if the media didn't try to hit you up for a personal interview," Damita dismally commented.

Terrell nodded in agreement. "They tried. When I got home this afternoon a local TV station's production truck was parked in front of the house. As I pulled into our driveway a reporter flung into action shouting questions, which categorically I refused to answer."

Megan's Fools Paradise

Damita made another drab assessment. "What's even worse is that we're the butt of church minister jokes by sinners and religious folk alike."

"That's why I can't wait to get away," Terrell interjected. "Glory to God. If it's the Lord's will my departure may be at hand."

"And so is our marriage. To phrase it differently; I would say, it's all but kaput."

"Your point of staying put is well taken too," Terrell followed.

"Oh really. Why the sudden change of mind?"

"I have been talking to God. Believe it or not. He agrees with you."

"So, He feel it's time for us to cut ties."

"Yes."

"Thank you, God!" Damita shouted.

Three weeks crept by since the shameful night Terrell was let go as the minister of Tabernacle Baptist. Terrell made his plans known to Damita as they once again sat around their dinner table.

"The Police Department of Los Angeles' Human Resources Department contacted me by phone earlier today with a proposal to come onboard as a fulltime officer, which I promptly accepted. I should receive an official letter noting my acceptance of the assignment by mail within a few days. My start date will be in exactly two weeks."

"So, your work for the Lord is done too."

"Not exactly. Once I'm settled in Los Angeles, I plan to start a Christian outreach program."

"How did you come up with that grandiose idea? Did you pray and ask God for guidance?"

"Yes, I did. During my visit to L.A. I met with Minister Travis Boatwright of The Los Angeles Devine Living Church. He stressed a need for clergy to aid an ever increasing under privileged/homeless population. Minister Boatwright was a classmate of mine at Harvey Ellis Christian Seminary."

"So, we will finally say our goodbyes," Damita sighed. "I wish you well."

ABOUT THE AUTHOR

Eddie Johnson is a native Floridian independent book author. His most recent works in the romance church drama genre are Megan's Fools Paradise, Dating a Single Minister, and Temptation in the Pulpit. And in the poetry genre his works are Reaching For Celestial Heights a collection of religious, and inspirational poems; and The Love of a Mother & Father a condensed selection of holiday and marital anniversary poems.

Throughout Eddie's life he's held jobs assisting others. He worked as a Public Assistance Specialist with the State of Florida for over a decade. Since then he has worked in private sector customer relations and billing related positions in telecommunications and banking. He has a Degree in Business Data Processing. Eddie is a devoted husband and father.

www.ingramcontent.com/pod-product-compliance
Lightning Source LLC
Chambersburg PA
CBHW071344130626

46556CB00005B/2013